For Porry,
May you discover the
courage that _is_
inside _you_!

Be brave!

Elaine Slade
x

ISBN: 978-1-8384003-1-6

A CIP catalogue record for this book is available from the British Library.

BOZ PUBLICATIONS

First published by Boz Publications Ltd 2021

Boz Publications Ltd.

71-75 Shelton Street, Covent Garden, London WC2H 9JQ

office@bozpublications.com - www.bozpublications.com

DON'T BE SCARED CHARLIE FARLEY!

Written by
Elaine Slade

Illustrated by
Monika Dzikowicz

Every year on Firework night,
Jasper gazed in sheer delight.

Whizz WHOOSH fizz POP!

How he wished
they would not stop.

Charlie Farley out of sight,
under the blanket crouched in fright.

BANG!

Hiss-ss-ss

Crackle

BOOM!

Fireworks meant doom and gloom.

DON'T BE SCARED
CHARLIE FARLEY!

He's not distressed
by lights flashing blue.

Sirens blaring through the town.
Terrified Charlie, cowering down.

NEE NAW!
NEE NAW! NEE NAW!
NEE NAW!!!

Ouch!
That made his
scruffy ears sore!

DON'T BE SCARED CHARLIE FARLEY!

Thunder, lightning lit up the sky.
Jasper calm as storm passes by.

Crash and bang, sudden downpour.
Snug in his bed, hear him snore.

Wind howled through the trees,
Charlie trembled, quivering knees!
Dark clouds rumbled, rage and roar.
Charlie could NOT stand anymore!

DON'T BE SCARED CHARLIE FARLEY!

Whilst Jasper calmly listened
with elegance and poise,
Charlie Farley detested
any loud noise.

He hung his head in shame,
what a sad matter.
Why was HE not
brave like Jasper?

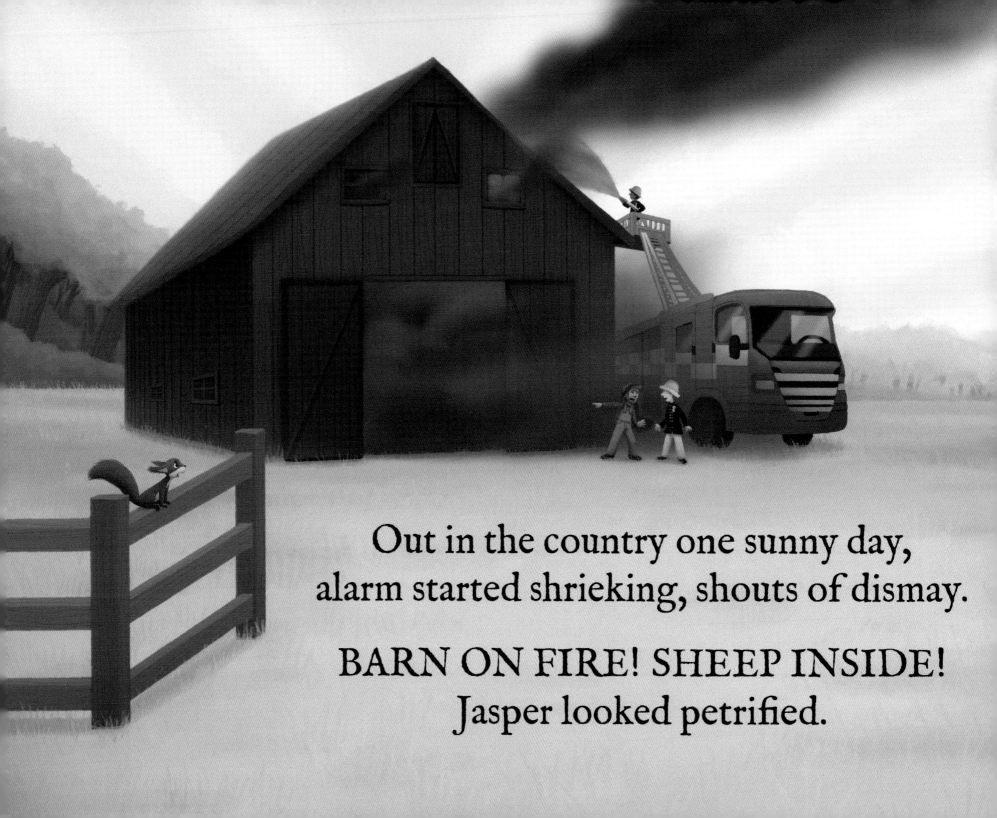

Out in the country one sunny day,
alarm started shrieking, shouts of dismay.

BARN ON FIRE! SHEEP INSIDE!
Jasper looked petrified.

In dashed Charlie, look at him go.
Fearlessly determined despite noise and glow.

He found the sheep, gently nudged them out.

His courage discovered, hear the people shout...

YOU'RE SO BRAVE CHARLIE FARLEY!

Charlie Farley was Jasper's brother,
DEAFENING noises made him shudder.
Yet, he had COURAGE in a disaster,
which made him just as BRAVE as Jasper.

Are there things that you're afraid of?
Find **COURAGE** like Charlie Farley
and discover the brave heart inside of YOU!

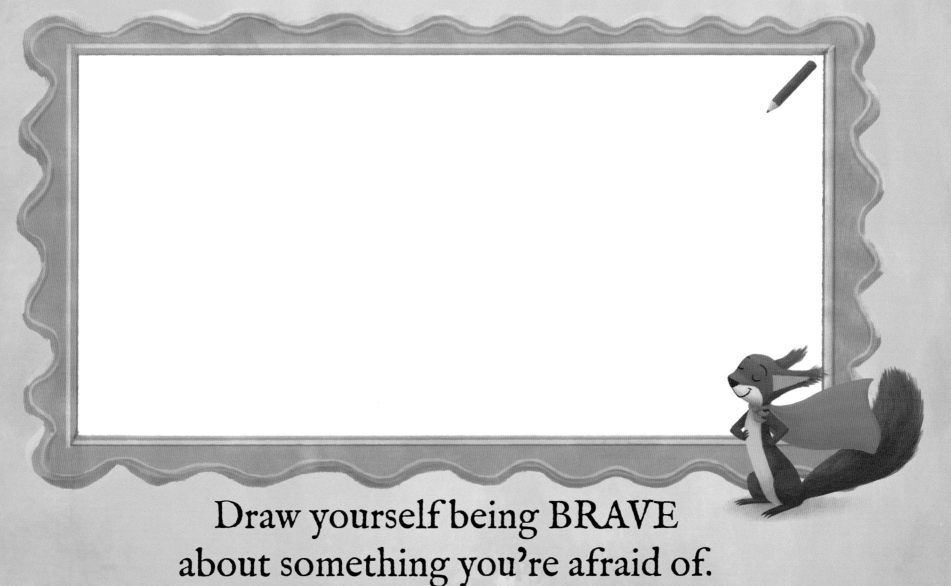

Draw yourself being BRAVE
about something you're afraid of.

HOW TO DRAW

1.

2.

3.

4.

5.

6.

7.

8.

9.

CHARLIE FARLEY

10.

11.

12.

13.

14.

LOOK!

CHARLIE FARLEY'S EXCITING ADVENTURES

DON'T BE SCARED CHARLIE FARLEY!

Written by
Elaine Slade

Illustrated by
Monika Dzikowicz

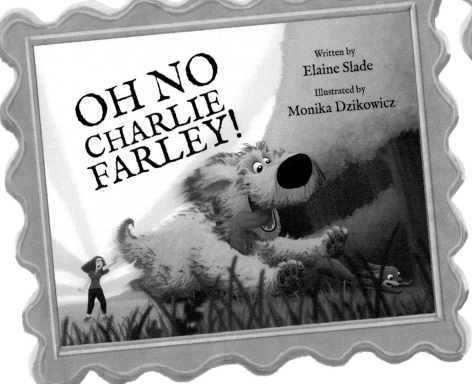

OH NO CHARLIE FARLEY!

Written by
Elaine Slade

Illustrated by
Monika Dzikowicz

AVAILABLE AT:

www.elainesladebooks.com

www.bozpublications.com

CHARLIE'S ACTIVITY GUIDE!
- Helping children talk through their fears and find the courage inside to face them -

Complete the page 'Are there things that you're afraid of?' together. Support your child/ren sensitively if they want to talk about something they find scary, always allow ideas to come from them.

Make an emotions chart to help identify feelings and what they look like; print a chart off the Internet or create your own photo scrapbook of family members miming different emotions.

Act out the story together using props e.g. model fire engine, toy sheep, blanket. Discuss how Charlie Farley is feeling in each scene, pointing out his facial expressions of emotion.

Take turns to mime emotions, the other person has to guess how their partner is feeling.

Look at words in the story that your child might not have understood e.g. crouched, poise, petrified, shudder. Look up the meaning together.

Explore the sound words in the story. Say them with expression and actions. Draw other words to reflect the noise they make e.g. buzz, squirt, jingle.

Make up a story about Charlie Farley facing a different fear and how he overcame it (often children will choose something they are afraid of as it reassures them that it can be overcome).

Draw a two-part picture showing before and after Charlie Farley has found the courage to face a fear.

Throughout your week ask your child once or twice how they are feeling about a situation; help them recognise their own emotions, how it makes their body feel and suggest ways to deal with fear e.g. count to ten, take deep breaths, 'the worst that could happen is...' and 'what would I do?'

Encourage your child to try something out of their comfort zone (not something they fear) whilst you are on hand to encourage and keep them safe e.g. climbing a tree, play equipment or a first-time visit. This teaches them to have confidence in other areas of life.

BRAVE HERO

JASPER'S MESSAGE TO PARENTS AND TEACHERS.

Before reading the book:

- What can you see on the front cover?
- How does Charlie Farley feel? Why does he feel like that?
- Does the blurb on the back tell us any more about the story?
- What do you think will happen to help Charlie Farley feel less scared?

Whilst reading the book:

- Can you help me find the little squirrel as we turn over each page?
- Encourage your child/ren to call out 'Don't be scared Charlie Farley!' and 'You're SO brave Charlie Farley!'
- Encourage your child/ren to say the 'sound' words themselves with actions e.g. BANG! hiss-ss-ss'
- *'DON'T BE SCARED CHARLIE FARLEY!'*: How is the little girl trying to make Charlie feel better? Is she scared?
- *'Police car chased along the street'*: Is Jasper scared of the Police car? Who is the little girl looking at?
- *'Sirens blaring through the town'*: Which words in the following text tell us that Charlie Farley was frightened?
- *'He hung his head in shame'*: Why did Charlie Farley do this?
- *'In dashed Charlie'*: Why is he dashing towards the loud noise and the fire? Isn't he scared?
- *'He found the sheep, gently nudged them out'*: What else does it say that Charlie Farley found?
- *'You're so brave Charlie Farley!'*: How does Charlie Farley feel? Why?
- Which part of the story did you like best? Why was that?

Questions to help explore facing fears and finding courage through the story:

- Which dog had the most courage, Jasper or Charlie Farley? Why?
- Talk about courage being different for different people. What scares you but doesn't scare your sibling/friend?
- Recall times when you or your child have faced fears and pushed through them with a positive outcome.
- How do we feel when we get past our fears? Praise your child for finding courage.
- Explain how the power of positive talking or thinking can help them push through their fears.

Elaine Slade - Author

Elaine is a former Deputy Head who loves exploring a good story and inspiring children, including her family (four daughters, two granddaughters) to love reading. She is passionate about raising children's self-esteem and teaching them to live life to the full. Elaine has overcome fears like Charlie Farley; she has trekked up to 4000m in the Himalayas and lived in Romania for three years.

www.elainesladebooks.com

Monika Dzikowicz - Illustrator

Monika, just like Charlie Farley, spent most of her childhood covered in mud; frolicking in nature; and looking up to her cool, older sister. When she grew up she embraced her uniqueness and became an illustrator who strives to visualise stories, which empower people and teach them emotional intelligence.

www.monikadzikowicz.com

To my husband Phil who always encourages me that I have the courage inside to face things I feel afraid of. Also to my daughters Becky and Abi who helped me face my fear of heights when trekking up the Himalayas.

Elaine Slade

Meet the REAL
Charlie Farley and Jasper.

Thanks to my husband for supporting me in being the best version of myself, and to my sister for showing me how to be strong and generous.

Monika Dzikowicz